NICK PAYNE

CONSTELLATIONS

Nick Payne is the author of *If There Is I Haven't Found It Yet* (Bush Theatre, London, and Roundabout Theatre Company, New York; winner of the 2009 George Devine Award for Most Promising Playwright), *Wanderlust* (Royal Court Theatre, London), an adaptation of Sophocles' *Electra* (Gate Theatre, London), *Lay Down Your Cross* (Hampstead Theatre Downstairs, London), *The Same Deep Water As Me* (Donmar Warehouse, London; nominated for a 2014 Laurence Olivier Award as Best New Comedy), *Blurred Lines* (The Shed, National Theatre, London), and *Incognito* (Bush Theatre, London). In London, *Constellations* was staged at the Royal Court Theatre and the Duke of York's Theatre. It was the winner of the 2012 Evening Standard Theatre Award for Best Play and was nominated for a 2013 Laurence Olivier Award as a MasterCard Best New Play.

CONSTELLATIONS

CONSTELLATIONS

NICK PAYNE

FARRAR, STRAUS AND GIROUX

NEW YORK

Farrar, Straus and Giroux
18 West 18th Street, New York 10011

Printed in the United States of America
Originally published in 2012 by Faber and Faber Ltd., Great Britain
Published in the United States by Farrar, Straus and Giroux
First American edition, 2014

Library of Congress Cataloging-in-Publication Data
Payne, Nick.
    Constellations / Nick Payne. — First American edition.
    pages ; cm.
    ISBN 978-0-86547-771-1 (pbk.)
    1. Interpersonal relations—Drama.   I. Title.

PR6116.A97 C66 2014
822'.92—dc23

                                        2013014939

Our books may be purchased in bulk for promotional, educational, or business
use. Please contact your local bookseller or the Macmillan Corporate
and Premium Sales Department at 1-800-221-7945, extension 5442, or by
e-mail at MacmillanSpecialMarkets@macmillan.com.

www.fsgbooks.com
www.twitter.com/fsgbooks • www.facebook.com/fsgbooks

10 9 8 7 6 5 4 3

For Minna
Dedicated to Dad

ACKNOWLEDGEMENTS

Chris Campbell, Jim Carnahan, Dominic Cooke, Lucy Cullingford, Lee Curran, Lucy Davies, Vicky Featherstone, Simon Godwin, Jake Gyllenhaal, Daisy Haggard, Sally Hawkins, Kate Horton, Mike Longhurst, Annie MacRae, David McSeveny, Lynne Meadow, Tom Scutt, Simon Slater, Rafe Spall, Vanessa Stone, Catherine Thornborrow, Evanna White, Ruth Wilson, all of the staff at Manhattan Theatre Club and all of the staff at the Royal Court Theatre.

Professor John D. Barrow, Steve Benbow, Cancer Research UK's Information Nurses, Professor Mike Duff, Dr John Gribbin, Professor Andrew Liddle, Silvan Luley and Ludwig A. Minelli (Dignitas), Duncan Macmillan, Dave Moore, Dr Kathy Romer and Charlie Swinbourne.

Ben Hall and Lily Williams at Curtis Brown and John Buzzetti at WME.

Mum.

I would like to acknowledge the following books and their authors: *On Being* by Peter Atkins, *The End of Time* by Julian Barbour, *The Book of Universes* by John D. Barrow, *From Eternity to Here* by Sean Carroll, *Beekeeping* by Andrew Davies, *Sum* by David Eagleman, *The Immortalization Commission* by John Gray, *The Elegant Universe* and *The Hidden Reality* by Brian Greene, *In Search of the Multiverse* by John Gribbin, *The Memory Chalet* by Tony Judt, *The Oxford Companion to Cosmology* by Andrew Liddle and John Loveday, *Quantum Theory: A Very Short Introduction* by John Polkinghorne and *The Trouble with Physics* by Lee Smolin.

Lastly, I would like to acknowledge 'A Memoir of Living with a Brain Tumour' by Tom Lubbock, originally published in *The Observer*, November 2010.

CONSTELLATIONS

Constellations had its world premiere at the Royal Court Jerwood Theatre Upstairs, Sloane Square, London, on January 13, 2011.

MARIANNE   Sally Hawkins
ROLAND   Rafe Spall

DIRECTOR   Michael Longhurst
DESIGNER   Tom Scutt
LIGHTING DESIGNER   Lee Curran
COMPOSER   Simon Slater
SOUND DESIGNER   David McSeveney
CASTING DIRECTOR   Amy Ball
ASSISTANT DIRECTOR   Sam Caird
PRODUCTION MANAGER   Tariq Rifaat
BSLBT CONSULTANT   Daryl Jackson
STAGE MANAGERS   Rhiannon Harper, Bryan Paterson
STAGE MANAGEMENT WORK PLACEMENT   Amy Burkett
COSTUME SUPERVISOR   Iona Kenrick

The American premiere of *Constellations* was produced by the Manhattan Theatre Club (Lynne Meadow, Artistic Director; Barry Grove, Executive Producer) and the Royal Court Theatre, by special arrangement with Ambassador Theatre Group and the Dodgers, at the Samuel J. Friedman Theatre. The first performance was on December 16, 2014.

MARIANNE   Ruth Wilson
ROLAND   Jake Gyllenhaal

DIRECTOR   Michael Longhurst
SCENIC AND COSTUME DESIGNER   Tom Scutt
LIGHTING DESIGNER   Lee Curran
SOUND DESIGNER   David McSeveney
MOVEMENT DIRECTOR   Lucy Cullingford
ORIGINAL MUSIC   Simon Slater
CASTING   Jim Carnahan and Nancy Piccione
STAGE MANAGER   Peter Wolf

CHARACTERS

Marianne
Roland

The reductionist worldview *is* chilling and impersonal. It has to be accepted as it is, not because we like it, but because that is the way the world works.

Steven Weinberg in Brian Greene,
The Elegant Universe

Science continues to be a channel for magic – the belief that for the human will, empowered by knowledge, nothing is impossible. This confusion of science with magic is not an ailment of a kind that has a remedy. It goes with modern life. Death is a provocation to this way of living, because it marks a boundary beyond which the will cannot go.

John Gray, *The Immortalization Commission*

Why should the universe have a purpose? The question of the purpose of the universe is an invention of human minds, and has no significance, except for the way that it illuminates the psychology of scholarly pursuit and of the pursuing scholars themselves. We should not impose human-inspired attitudes and questions on material things. There is a considerable grandeur, I think, in the presence of our spectacularly majestic universe just hanging there, wholly without purpose.

Peter Atkins, *On Being*

An indented rule indicates a change in universe.

Marianne Do you know why it's impossible to lick the tips of your elbows? They hold the secret to immortality, so if you could lick them, there's a chance you'd be able to live forever. But if everyone did it, if everyone could actually lick the tips of their elbows, then there'd be chaos. Because you can't just go on living and living and living.

Roland I'm. I'm in a relationship. So. Yeah.

———————————

Marianne Do you know why it's impossible to lick the tips of your elbows? They hold the secret to immortality, so if you could lick them, there's a chance you'd be able to live forever. But if everyone did it, if everyone could actually lick the tips of their elbows, then there'd be chaos. Because you can't just go on living and living and living.

Roland I've. I've just come out of a really serious relationship. So. Yeah.

Marianne I was just making conversation.

Roland Sure.

Marianne Just trying to start a conversation.

Roland No, sure. But. Still.

———————————

Marianne Do you know why it's impossible to lick the tips of your elbows? They hold the secret to immortality, so if you could lick them, there's a chance you'd be able

9

to live forever. But if everyone did it, if everyone could actually lick the tips of their elbows, then there'd be chaos. Because you can't just go on living and living and living.

Roland Oh right.

Marianne Try it.

Roland What's that?

Marianne Your elbows, try licking them.

Roland I'm all right.

Marianne attempts to lick her elbows, demonstrating the difficulty.

Marianne I'm Marianne.

Roland Roland.

Marianne Thank God the rain's held off.

Roland Yeah.

Marianne Nothing worse than a soggy barbecue.

Roland Yeah.

Marianne Soggy sausages. Would you like a drink?

Roland I'm all right. My wife's actually just gone to get me a beer.

Marianne Try it.

Roland What's that?

Marianne Your elbows, try licking them.

Marianne attempts to lick her elbows, demonstrating the difficulty. Roland, initially hesitant, also attempts to lick his elbows.

Roland See what you mean. I'm Roland.

Marianne Marianne.

Roland Shame about the rain.

Marianne Nothing worse than a soggy barbecue.

Roland So are you, are you a friend of Jane's or –

Marianne No, Jane, yeah. We were at college together.

Roland Right.

Marianne Yourself?

Roland My wife used to work with Jane.

––––––––––––––––

Marianne Your elbows, try licking them.

Marianne attempts to lick her elbows, demonstrating the difficulty. Roland, initially hesitant, also attempts to lick his elbows.

Roland See what you mean. I'm Roland.

Marianne Marianne.

Roland Shame about the rain.

Marianne Nothing worse than a soggy barbecue.

Roland So are you, are you a friend of Jane's or . . . ?

Marianne Who's Jane?

Roland Jane's the – She's the lady having the barbecue?

Marianne Oh, right, Christ, no. I was just walking past and I saw a load of free booze and sausages. I'm joking.

Roland Right.

Marianne Jane and I were at college together. How about you?

Roland I play football with Tom.

Marianne Tom?

Roland Jane's brother-in-law. Bluey-green T-shirt.

Marianne Yes.

Roland D'you want a drink?

Marianne I'm fine. Thanks.

Roland So what do you, what do you do? For a living.

Marianne I work at Sussex University.

Roland Right. Great.

Marianne Yourself?

Roland I'm a beekeeper.

Marianne Really?

Roland Yeah, yeah.

Marianne You're really a beekeeper?

Roland I'm really a beekeeper.

Marianne I fucking love honey.

Roland Oh really?

Marianne Spoon. Jar of honey. Heaven.

Roland What sort of honey do you normally go for?

Marianne I'm too embarrassed.

Roland How d'you mean?

Marianne Too embarrassed to tell you.

Roland Why's that?

*Marianne whispers the following into Roland's ear:
'I like Tesco. The really dirty stuff, the prison stripe
stuff.'*

Roland That's all right.

Marianne Really?

Roland Of course.

Marianne I'm not putting honest, hard-working beekeepers out of business?

Roland Wouldn't've thought so.

Marianne Do you think I'm a honey philistine?

Roland Some of the supermarket stuff's all right.

Marianne Really?

Roland Yeah, some of it's fine, yeah.

Marianne So – And I mean don't take this the wrong way, but, I mean, are you –

Roland Go on.

Marianne You – I mean do you make a living?

Roland I do, yeah.

Marianne I mean from beekeeping.

Roland From beekeeping.

Marianne How does it – I mean how does it –

Roland Well. I used to, I used to work for a friend of mine. In Wiltshire.

Marianne Very nice.

Roland After a while though, decided I wanted to go into business on my own. But my, my girlfriend – ex-girlfriend –

Marianne I'm sorry for your loss.

Roland What's that?

Marianne No – I was – I was making a –

Roland Right.

Marianne Sorry for your loss as in –

Gestures, sliding a finger across her throat, 'killed'.

Roland Right.

Marianne It was just a –

Roland No.

Marianne Anyway, you were –

Roland Yeah, no, so, she, my ex, she wanted to move to London. So we got this one-bed place in Tower Hamlets.

Marianne No wonder you broke up with her, fuck me. I'd've broken up with her if she'd made me leave Wiltshire for fucking Tower Hamlets.

Roland I'm still living there, actually.

Marianne Lovely curries.

Roland There wasn't any room. For bees.

Marianne I see.

Roland We didn't have a garden.

Marianne Bummer.

Roland One day I was up on the roof and I realised it was perfect. So I tidied it up a bit and I got my first hive.

Marianne Amazing.

Roland Went from one to two from two to four. We, we went away. Me and Laura. We went away to Spain and when we got back, we found that the flat had been raided.

Marianne Raided?

Roland I used to keep the honey in bin bags. You know those black, plastic bin liners –

Marianne Yes.

Roland Didn't have a lotta money, at the time, so the bin bags were just a cheap alternative. When we were away though, one of the neighbours called the police. Thought I was brewing up smack or something. They properly went for it. The police. They kicked the front door in, turned the flat upside down and they confiscated all these bin bags filled with the most amazing honey and honeycomb.

Marianne Did that really happen?

Roland Yeah.

Marianne You used to keep honey in bin bags?

Roland Yeah.

Marianne *Roland, I don't think that I can go back to work.*

Roland *Have they told you that?*

Marianne *They're great.*

Roland *You've told them then?*

Marianne *Not yet.*

Roland *But you're going to.*

Marianne *I think so.*

Roland *But you haven't said any of this to them?*

Marianne *They've said whatever I want.*

Roland *So what about part-time?*

Marianne *I don't know the point.*

Roland *You mean the point of going part-time?*

Marianne *Either I'm walking or I'm*

Either I'm   walker

I either do it or I don't. Scares me.

Roland *Work?*

Marianne *Stopping.*

Roland *Stopping work scares you?*

Marianne *What will I do?*

Roland *We'll go away. We can do whatever we want.*

Marianne *I don't –*

Roland *I'm being serious.*

Marianne *I don't –*

Roland *I mean it.*

Marianne *I   I don't*

We can't. I have to   have to   make a

I have to have a choice.

Control.

Roland You want me to leave?

Marianne Not in a bad way, but yeah.

Roland Have I done something wrong?

Marianne No.

Roland Have I said something, have I offended you?

Marianne No.

Roland I thought we'd had a nice evening?

Marianne We did.

Roland Coming back here was your suggestion?

Marianne I know, but, on reflection –

Roland Do you wanna come inside, you said.

Marianne I know I know, but now I've changed my mind. I'm allowed to change my mind, aren't I?

Roland If I'm allowed to ask why, sure.

Marianne I just – I'd just rather not get into it.

Roland Can you at least tell me if it's me?

Marianne I just –

Roland I'm not saying specifically – Generally – Generally speaking –

Marianne I'm just going through some things. At the moment. And you're right, we've had a lovely evening and you're right it was my idea to come back here, but, I just, as soon as we stepped inside, I started thinking – I mean I just started thinking –

_____

Roland You want me to leave?

Marianne Not in a bad way, but yeah.

Roland Have I done something wrong?

Marianne No.

Roland Have I said something, have I offended you?

Marianne No.

17

Roland Then I don't understand?

Marianne I'm not asking you to understand, I'm asking you to leave.

Roland Bit fucking rich, isn't it?

Marianne I'm sorry?

Roland This was your idea.

Marianne Charming.

Roland I'm just saying.

Marianne Okay –

Roland It's rude.

Marianne Yeah I'd like you to leave now.

Roland I should probably make a move.

Marianne You don't – I mean don't feel you have to.

Roland I've got a really early start.

Marianne How early's early?

Roland Six.

Marianne You could – I mean you could – Not in a like 'welcome to my lair' way or anything, but – If you wanted, you could. Stay.

Roland I should probably head back.

Marianne Well, look, I mean – Thanks for a really lovely evening.

Roland Likewise, yeah.

Marianne We should – I mean whenever you're free, we should think about –

Roland Definitely, yeah.

Marianne The 'lair' thing was just a joke by the way.

Roland Come again?

Marianne Sofa just folds out. You wouldn't have to stay in my bed. Stop talking, Marianne.

Roland gently kisses Marianne 'goodbye' on the cheek.

Marianne Not in a bad way, but yeah.

Roland Have I done something wrong?

Marianne No.

Roland Have I said something –

Marianne No.

Roland I thought we'd had a nice evening?

Marianne We did.

Roland Coming back here was your suggestion?

Marianne No, I know, but, on reflection –

Roland Do you wanna come inside, you said.

Marianne I know, but now I've changed my mind. I'm allowed to change my mind, aren't I? I just – I'd just rather not get into it.

Roland I went on another date a couple of weeks ago. Almost exactly the same thing happened. So I'm more than happy to leave you to it, but if it is me –

Marianne It's not.

Roland I'm not saying you have to be specific –

Marianne It's not you.

Roland If you had some feedback –

Marianne Feedback?

Roland 'Feedback''s not right, but –

Marianne Okay, look, I just. I'm just going through some things. At the moment. My, my mother. She's been ill for a really long time. And. I can't tell whether I want you to stay because I want you to stay or whether I just don't want to go to sleep on my own.

Beat.

Roland I'm really sorry.

Marianne Why don't we just speak in a week or so?

Marianne and Roland are a little drunk.

Roland Friend of mine said to me when I told him that I was going on a date, he said, 'What does she do?' –

Marianne And what did you say?

Roland I said I don't really know but I think it's something to do with space. And when we were talking about your job earlier on I was nodding along pretty much the entire time but when we stepped through your front door I realised I hadn't really understood a single thing you'd said.

Marianne Most of my time is spent sitting in front of a computer.

Roland Right.

Marianne Inputting data.

Roland Right.

Marianne Cosmic microwave background readings.

Roland Okay.

Marianne Radiation left over from the big bang.

Roland Right.

Marianne Cosmology. Theoretical early universe cosmology.

Marianne and Roland are a little more drunk.

Roland I said I don't really know but I think it's something to do with space. And when we were talking about your job earlier on I was nodding along pretty much the entire time but when we stepped through your front door I realised I hadn't really understood a single thing you'd said.

Marianne Most of my time is spent sitting in front of a computer.

Roland Right.

Marianne Inputting data.

Roland Right.

Marianne Quantum cosmology.

Roland Right.

Marianne Do you know much about theoretical physics?

Roland Pass.

Marianne Quantum mechanics?

Roland Pass.

Marianne Quantum mechanics focuses on the quantum realm. Atoms, molecules.

Roland Right.

Marianne On nuclear and atomic scales, gravity is pretty much insignificant. But in terms of General Relativity, it's vital.

Roland Okay.

Marianne So you've these two theories that are completely at odds with one another. Relativity covers the sun, the moon, the stars, while quantum mechanics takes care of molecules, quarks, atoms – that sort of thing. We've effectively asked the same question twice and come up with two completely different answers.

Roland This is really sexy by the way.

Marianne The point being –

Roland I had a really amazing time tonight and I'd really like to spend the night.

Marianne But –

Roland With you. I'd really like to spend the night –

Marianne But now we've got string theory. Or, to be a bit more specific, we've got lots of different string theories –

Roland If you'd rather I didn't stay you just have to say.

Marianne And the exciting thing about string theory is that it potentially bridges the gap between relativity and –

Roland You haven't answered either of my questions.

Marianne kisses Roland.

Marianne A by-product of every single one of these theories – almost entirely by accident – is the possibility that we're part of a multiverse.

Roland kisses Marianne.

Despite our best efforts, there are certain microscopic observations that just cannot be predicted absolutely.

Now, potentially, one way of explaining this is to draw the conclusion that, at any given moment, several outcomes can co-exist simultaneously.

Roland This is genuinely turning me on, you do realise that?

Marianne In the quantum multiverse, every choice, every decision you've ever and never made exists in an unimaginably vast ensemble of parallel universes.

Roland Everything?

Marianne Everything.

Roland Everything I've ever done?

Marianne Everything you've ever and never done. We should try and keep our voices down, my housemate –

Roland But if everything I'm ever gonna do already exists, then what's the point in me –

Marianne Well –

Roland What's the point in me even –

Marianne Well –

Roland D'you see what I'm saying?

Marianne No, totally, but – Let's say that ours really is the only universe that exists. There's only one unique me and one unique you. If that were true, then there could only ever really be one choice. But if every possible future exists, then the decisions we do and don't make will determine which of these futures we actually end up experiencing. Imagine rolling a dice six thousand times.

Still drunk.

Roland Everything?

Marianne Everything.

Roland Everything I've ever done?

Marianne Everything you've ever and never done. We should try and keep our voices down, my housemate –

Roland But if everything I'm ever gonna do already exists, then what's the point in me –

Marianne There isn't.

Roland What?

Marianne In none of our equations do we see any sign whatsoever of any evidence of free will.

Roland In your e—

Marianne We're just particles.

Roland Speak for y'self.

Marianne You, me, everyone, we might think that we have some say in – We might *think* that the choices we make will have some say in the –

Roland Right, no, sure –

Marianne We're just particles –

Roland No, sure, but –

Marianne We're just particles governed by a series of very particular laws being knocked the fuck around all over the place.

Roland You make it sound so glamorous.

––––––––––––––––––––––

Marianne and Roland are sober.

Marianne Most of my time is spent sitting in front of a

24

computer typing in numbers. It's not really very interesting.

Roland Okay.

Marianne Look. I, I've had a really enjoyable evening.

Roland No, yeah, me –

Marianne I haven't really made up my mind, though, whether or not I'd like you to stay. I just – I've got quite a bit on at the moment and we were having a really lovely time and I thought it would be really nice to invite you back. But I just want to be clear that I'm not massively interested in sleeping with you.

Roland It's all right, you don't have to –

Marianne I'd just sort of rather get into bed and go to sleep. But I'm completely happy to go and get you a sleeping bag and a couple of towels.

Roland Okay.

Marianne But – I mean, just to be clear, I'm not being coy. I'm not sort of saying no to sex but yes to all the other stuff. We're going to go to sleep, separately, and then we're going to wake up and then we're going to have some toast. Or, I mean, whatever. You don't have to have toast.

Roland Floor's fine. Honestly.

Marianne *I'm so tired. I'm so tired, Roland. Before people had face*

Before they had   face

Face   before they

FUCK.

Roland *Okay.*

Marianne *God.*

Roland *God?*

Marianne *People's lives were their own. Before   it became skin*

Skin, it became

Skin

Roland *Skin?*

Marianne *Mum wasn't scared of dying, she was scared of being kept alive. You know?*

Roland *Yes.*

Marianne *That wasn't what scared her.*

Roland *I understand.*

Marianne *It's not just the speaking.*

Roland *Okay now I don't understand?*

Marianne *Reading. I'm having trouble – Numbers, words, on the page. I don't know how to explain it. Typing. Typing, as well.*

Roland *In what way?*

Marianne *I know the word. I know the word I'm trying to type. But I don't know the letters. None of the letters seem right. Rea*

Rea

Rea

Roland *You don't need to finish.*

Marianne *I want to.*

Roland *I think I know what you're trying to say.*

Marianne *How   How can you know what I'm trying to say?*

Mmm   Most of the time I don't even know what I'm trying to say.

Roland *You're right I was being polite because I don't want you to wear yourself out.*

Marianne *Maybe we should get me a notepad to hang around my neck?*

Roland *What?*

Marianne *Kidding.*

Roland *Mary fucking hell.*

Marianne *Roland, I don't think that I can go back to work.*

Roland All right?

Marianne Where have you been?

Roland Pub.

Marianne I sent you a text.

Roland I know.

Marianne Why didn't you text me back?

Roland Dunno.

Marianne What does that mean?

Roland It means I dunno. Means I didn't think it was urgent.

Marianne I didn't know where you were.

Roland I just told you.

Marianne Now, you just told me now, but I wanted to know –

Roland I was playing tennis. I was playing tennis with Tony and then we went to the pub. What's wrong? I'm sorry. What is it, what's wrong?

Marianne Roland, I'm really sorry.

Roland What, what is it?

Marianne James and I had sex.

Roland James.

Marianne From work.

Roland The centre parting? You mean the bloke with the centre parting?

Marianne Yes.

Roland When?

Marianne We've – There's been a few. A few times.

Roland How many's a few?

Marianne I'd rather we didn't get into who did what to whom.

Roland How many's a few, Mary?

Marianne Six. Maybe seven.

Roland Spread out? Were the six or seven times you had sex spread out over a particular period of time?

Marianne Yes.

Roland Are you together, then, d'you wanna be together?

Marianne I don't know.

Roland Is he moving in?

Marianne Of course not. Roland, of course he's not.

Roland Do you want me to move out?

  Beat.

When do you want me to move out?

Marianne There's no rush.

Roland That's it then is it?

Marianne Where have you been?

Roland Pub.

Marianne I sent you a text.

Roland I know.

Marianne Why didn't you text me back?

Roland Dunno.

Marianne What does that mean?

Roland It means I dunno. Means I didn't think it was urgent.

Marianne I didn't know where you were.

Roland I just told you.

Marianne Now, you just told me now, but I wanted to know –

Roland I was playing tennis. I was playing tennis with Tony and then we went to the pub. What's wrong? I'm sorry. What is it, what's wrong?

Marianne Roland, I'm really sorry.

Roland What, what is it?

Marianne James and I had sex.

Roland James.

Marianne From work.

Roland Dandruff? You mean the bloke with the dandruff?

Marianne He doesn't – Yes.

Roland When?

Marianne We've – There's been a few. A few times.

Roland How many's a few?

Marianne I'd rather we didn't get into who did what to whom.

Roland How many's a few, Mary?

Marianne Six. Maybe seven.

Roland Spread out?

Marianne What?

Roland Were the six or seven times you had sex spread out over a particular period of time?

Marianne Yes.

Roland Are you together, then, d'you wanna be together? Mary, do the two of you –

Marianne I don't know.

Roland Is he moving in?

   Beat.

When do you want me to move out?

Marianne There's no rush.

Roland How old is he?

Marianne He's twenty-four.

Roland Twenty-four?

Marianne Yes.

Roland He's a child.

Marianne He's twenty-four, Roland.

Roland Where do you have sex?

Marianne All sorts of places.

Roland Fuck does that mean?

Marianne It's means we've had sex in more than one place.

Roland Here?

Marianne Roland, of course we've not had –

Roland His place?

Marianne Yes.

Roland Where does he live?

Marianne Brighton.

Roland You have sex in the daytime then?

Marianne Yes.

Roland In the fucking daytime?

Marianne Sometimes, yes.

Roland During lunch is it?

Beat.

So when's he gonna move in? Mary, when's he gonna –

Marianne There's no date.

Roland But he is gonna move in?

Marianne Hopefully.

Roland Am I boring?

Marianne What?

Roland Do I bore you?

Marianne Of course not.

Roland We don't talk about space enough, is that it?

Marianne It's nothing to do with work.

Roland That doesn't make it better, y'know. If you'd said yes, if you'd said yes, it's because we don't talk about space enough, it might have made a bit more sense. I'd kick myself for not making more of an effort, but at least it'd make a bit more sense.

Marianne There's no linear explanation I'm afraid.

Roland Where have you been?

Marianne Work.

Roland I sent you a text.

Marianne I know.

Roland You've not texted me back?

Marianne I know.

Roland What does that mean?

Marianne It means I know that you sent me a text.

Roland I didn't know where you were.

Marianne Why are you being so tetchy? I was at work and I missed the seven thirty-seven and then the eight oh-four didn't turn up. What's wrong, what's the matter?

Roland Mary I'm really sorry but I had sex with Alison O'Connor Tuesday the week before last.

Marianne Alison O'Connor.

Roland Yeah.

Marianne I thought she was going bald?

Roland What?

Marianne She's going bald, Roland, she's going fucking bald. Well how many times? How many times did you have sex with her, Roland?

Roland Once.

Marianne Once?

Roland Tuesday the week before last, yeah.

Marianne What were you doing, what were the two of you doing?

Roland I was helping her set up a hive.

Marianne Is this a fucking joke?

Roland No.

Marianne You were helping her set up a fucking *hive*?

Roland Yes.

Marianne Speak up.

Roland I said yes. Yes, I was helping her –

Marianne Is it serious?

Roland I don't know.

Marianne You don't know?

Roland I need some time to think about it.

Marianne Oh you need some time to think about it?

Roland Preferably, yes.

Beat.

Marianne Does this mean you're moving out?

Roland Up to you, really.

Marianne If it were up to me, Roland, you wouldn't have fucked fucking Alison O'Connor.

Roland All right.

Marianne I beg your pardon?

Roland Calm down.

Marianne Fuck you actually.

Beat.

I've never been happier. Living with you. Just so you know.

Roland That doesn't make it better, y'know. If you'd said yes, if you'd said yes, it's because we don't talk about space enough, it might have made a bit more sense. I'd kick myself for not making more of an effort, but at least it'd make a bit more sense.

Marianne There's no straightforward explanation I'm afraid.

Roland Don't make me leave.

Marianne Roland –

Roland This is the best fucking thing that's ever happened to me, I'm serious.

Marianne You'll be fine.

Roland I don't know what I'm gonna do.

Marianne You can move back to Tower Hamlets.

Roland Is that meant to be a joke?

Marianne Of course it's not. I just meant that you've got lots – There's lots you can do.

Roland I don't care.

Marianne Come on.

Roland I don't.

Marianne You're being melodramatic.

Roland How long have you been waiting to tell me?

Marianne A week.

Roland I was going to propose.

Marianne Roland –

Roland I need some time to think about it.

Marianne Oh you need some time to think about it?

Roland Preferably, yes.

   Beat.

Marianne Does this mean you're moving out?

Roland Up to you, really.

Marianne If it were up to me, Roland, you wouldn't have fucked fucking –

Roland All right.

Marianne I beg your pardon?

Roland I don't wanna fight.

Marianne Tough.

Roland What?

Marianne I said tough.

Roland Mary, come on, I'm telling you because I regret it, not because I want us to –

Marianne You regret something once; you don't regret it and then keep going.

Roland What's the likelihood you might be able to forgive me?

Marianne Where have you been?

Roland Pub.

Marianne I sent you a text.

Roland I know.

Marianne Why didn't you text me back?

Roland Dunno.

Marianne What does that mean?

Roland It means I dunno. Means I didn't think it was urgent.

Marianne I didn't know where you were.

Roland I just told you.

Marianne Now, you just told me now, but I wanted to know –

Roland I was playing tennis. I was playing tennis with Tony and then we went to the pub. What's wrong? I'm sorry. What is it, what's wrong?

Marianne Roland, I'm really sorry.

Roland What, what is it?

Marianne James and I had sex.

Beat.

Marianne Roland, did you hear what I –

Roland I know.

Marianne What?

Roland You had a message from him while you were in the shower. I read it.

Roland hits Marianne. Beat.

Marianne Yeah you need to leave.

Roland Make me.

Marianne What?

Roland I said make me.

Marianne *I keep thinking of Mum.*

Roland *In what way?*

Marianne *Before she died.*

Roland *Right.*

Marianne *When she said she didn't want any more food.*

Roland *Yeah.*

Marianne *Do you remember?*

Roland *I'm not sure we ever really talked about it?*

Marianne *I thought we did?*

Roland *Bits and pieces maybe.*

Marianne *Well she said she wanted them to stop the IV, did we talk about that?*

37

Roland *I think maybe we did yeah.*

Marianne *They asked me to leave. I went back the next day and she was starting to look like a ghost. It takes an enormous amount of strength. When you're like that. To keep going. I'm not sure I have it.*

Roland *You don't know. You don't know that.*

Marianne *Sinking feeling.*

Roland *Mary listen to me –*

Marianne *I'm so tired. I'm so tired, Roland. Before people had face*

Before they had   face

Face   before they

FUCK.

Roland *Okay.*

Marianne *God.*

Roland *God?*

Marianne *People's lives were their own. Before   it became skin*

Skin, it became

Skin

Roland *Skin?*

Marianne *Mum wasn't scared of dying, she was scared of being kept alive. You know?*

Roland *Yes.*

Marianne *That wasn't what scared her.*

Roland Hello, Marianne.

Marianne Roland. Wow, hi – Hello. How are you?

Roland Yeah, I'm fine, thanks.

Marianne Oh good. Good, that's really good.

Roland How about y'self?

Marianne I bought some of your honey.

Roland Oh really.

Marianne From the Budgens in Crouch End.

Roland Yeah, right. They're really great.

Marianne I said to the girl on the till, I said I used to know the man who made this honey.

Roland What did she say?

Marianne . . .

Roland I read one of your papers.

Marianne You did not?

Roland I did. I downloaded it.

Marianne Which one did you read?

Roland Something to do with the XMM Cluster Survey?

Marianne That's really amazing, Roland.

Roland What did you think of the honey?

Marianne Delicious. It was completely delicious. Are you, are you here for the ballroom class?

Roland Yeah, no, yeah, I am, yeah.

Marianne Really.

Roland Heather's getting married in a couple of months, so.

Marianne The PE teacher?

Roland What's that?

Marianne He was a, he was a PE teacher, wasn't he?

Roland Right, no, I see. They called it a day. New bloke's a something-or-other for the Office for National Statistics.

Marianne Wow.

Roland I've been ordered to sort out my two left feet or else. How about you?

Marianne Similar, really. Wedding.

Roland Your own or –

Marianne No, mine, yep.

Roland Congratulations.

Marianne Yep.

Roland Is your. Fiancé, is he –

Marianne Held up. He's. Been held up.

Roland Hello, Marianne. It's Roland.

Marianne Roland.

Roland How are you? Hope I didn't scare you?

Marianne No. A bit. Maybe. I mean, a bit.

Roland Sorry.

Marianne Are you, are you here for the ballroom class?

Roland Yeah, no, yeah, I am, yeah.

Marianne Ballroom, really?

Roland Heather's getting married.

Marianne Heather?

Roland My sister.

Marianne Heather, of course.

Roland I've been ordered to sort out my two left feet or else.

Marianne Did you, did you know that I was going to be here?

Roland What? Did I –

Marianne Know that I was going to be here?

Roland No. No, of course not.

  Beat.

Marianne I'm learning ballroom because I'm getting married, Roland.

Roland No, sure.

Marianne In September.

Roland Congratulations.

Marianne Thank you. What about you, are you –

Roland I was, but, for the moment, no.

Marianne Married?

Roland Seeing someone. I was seeing someone. But we broke up. So.

Marianne I'm sorry.

Roland No, please. Don't be.

Marianne Hello, Roland.

Roland Marianne. Wow, shit. How's it, how's it going?

Marianne Well. I'm really well. Thanks.

Roland Great. Thass really great.

Marianne Yourself?

Roland Yeah, no, I mean, good, yeah.

Marianne I bought some of your honey.

Roland Oh really.

Marianne From the Budgens in Crouch End.

Roland Yeah, right. They're really great.

Marianne I said to the girl on the till, I said I used to know the man who made this honey.

Roland What did she say?

Marianne She just stared at me. How is everything? Business-wise.

Roland Good, yeah. 'Bout to start doing pollen.

Marianne Pollen?

Roland Yeah, you have to – Y'scrape it off the legs of the bees and then you ground it down. Really good for you apparently.

Marianne Scraping the legs of bees, or pollen?

Roland Had a, had an offer from Tesco of all people.

Marianne For the pollen?

Roland No, just for the honey.

Marianne How much for?

Roland Fair whack.

Marianne What did you say?

Roland Told 'em to go fuck 'emselves. I read one of your papers.

Marianne You did not?

Roland I did. I downloaded it.

Marianne Which one did you read?

Roland Something about hot subdwarf stars?

Marianne Were you really looking for midget porn on Google?

Roland What's that?

Marianne Subdwarf – It was a –

Roland Gotcha.

Marianne That's really amazing, Roland. Thank you.

Roland What did you think of the honey? From Budgens.

Marianne Delicious. It was completely delicious.

Roland It's heather.

Marianne Yes.

Roland We cart the bees up to the heather moors every August. One by one.

Marianne One by one?

Roland Hives, not bees.

Marianne Are you, are you here for the ballroom class?

Roland Yeah, no, yeah, I am, yeah. I'm. I'm actually. Engaged.

Marianne Oh wow.

Roland So. Yeah.

Marianne Who's the, who's the lucky lady?

Roland Alison. Alison O –

Marianne I remember.

Roland How about y'self, are you –

Marianne Just trying to lose a bit of weight. Too many late-night digestive binges. I blame the subdwarfs. The stars – The, the paper you read –

Roland Heather's getting married in a couple of months, so.

Marianne The PE teacher?

Roland What's that?

Marianne He was a, he was a PE teacher, wasn't he?

Roland Right, no, I see. They called it a day. New bloke's a something-or-other for the DVLA.

Marianne Wow.

Roland I've been ordered to sort out my two left feet or else. How about you?

Marianne Similar, really. Wedding.

Roland Your own or –

Marianne No, God, can you imagine. I'm being a very diligent bridesmaid. We're having some kind of mass Viennese waltz. I'm not sure I fully understand it as yet.

Roland So is this your first? Lesson.

Marianne No, second. You?

Roland First, yeah.

Marianne Well done on the comfortable trouser front. I came straight from work. Last week. Crotch was like a fucking furnace by the time I got home.

44

Beat.

Roland Mary, I'm sorry.

Marianne Well done on the comfortable trouser front.
I came straight from work. Last week. Crotch was like a
fucking inferno by the time I got home.

Beat.

Roland, I'm sorry.

Roland What for?

Marianne Well done on the comfortable trouser front. I
came straight from work. Last week. Crotch was like a
fucking sauna by the time I got home.

Beat.

I have to say it because if I don't I'll feel like a fraud.

Roland Mary –

Marianne Let's go for a drink. I don't know what I'm
doing here anyway. One drink. And if you never want to
see me again you never have to see me again.

Roland Mary –

Marianne Why don't we go for a drink? I don't know
what I'm doing here anyway. One drink. And if you
never want to see me again you never have to see me
again.

Roland Mary –

Marianne One drink. And if you never want to see me again you never have to see me again.

Roland Mary –

Marianne And if you never want to see me again you never have to see me again.

Roland *I don't really know what to say.*

Marianne *You don't have to say anything.*

Roland *No I know but I want to; I want to know what to say to you.*

Marianne *A lot of people apparently never go through with it.*

Roland *How do you mean?*

Marianne *A lot of people, once they've been given the green night*

Night

Once they've   A lot of

Roland *It's okay.*

Marianne *They're, they're happy enough knowing it's there.*

Roland *How do you know that?*

Marianne *It's on the website.*

Roland *When you say 'a lot' how many are we talking?*

Marianne *I think it was something like two-thirds. Safety net. For a lot of people.*

Roland *And is that how you're feeling about it?*

Marianne *I don't know.*

Roland *Would I be able to come with you?*

Marianne *I'm going to speak to Martin. Would you want to? Come with me.*

Roland *Would you want me to come with you?*

   Marianne nods. Beat.

Marianne *I keep thinking of Mum.*

Roland takes a piece of A4 paper from a pocket and reads.

Roland There are three
different kinds of bees. The
drones, the workers and a
single, solitary queen. The
workers are all women. Their
job is to forage for honey,
pollen, etcetera. Their lifespan
is potentially anywhere
between five weeks and six
months. And then they die.
Drones exist solely to have
sex with the queen. Each hive
tends to have around a
hundred drones. Once they've
deposited their sperm, their
penis gets ripped off and
they die. Honeybees have an   **Marianne** Roland –
unfailing clarity of purpose.
Their lives are often intensely
short. But in a strange sort of
way, I'm jealous of the humble

47

honeybee and their quiet elegance. If only our existence were that simple. If only we could understand why it is that we're here and what it is that we're meant to spend our lives doing. I am uncertain when it comes to a great many things. But there is now one thing I am defiantly certain of.

Marianne Roland any moment a –

Marianne Any moment a –

Roland folds up the piece of paper, puts it back in his pocket and – from another pocket – takes out a small black box. He kneels and opens the small black box.

Roland Marianne Aubele, will you marry me?

Marianne Roland, I've got a tutorial. You can't just turn up like this. I mean. It's the middle of the day, there's a lot going on. I need to think about it. I'm sorry. I just. I just really need some space.

Roland stands and returns the small black box to his pocket.

———————————

Marianne This is a surprise.

Roland Is it?

Marianne It's the middle of the afternoon.

Roland Are you busy?

Marianne Are you – Is everything –

Roland There's something I'd like to say. To you.

Roland takes a piece of A4 paper from a pocket and reads.

There are three different kinds of bees. The drones, the workers and a single, solitary queen. The workers are all women. Their job is to forage for honey, pollen, etcetera. Their lifespan is potentially anywhere between five weeks and six months. And then they die. Drones exist solely to have sex with the queen. Each hive tends to have around a hundred drones. Once they've deposited their sperm, their penis gets ripped off and they die. Honeybees have an unfailing clarity of purpose. Their lives are often intensely short. But in a strange sort of way, I'm jealous of the humble honeybee and their quiet elegance. If only our existence were that simple. If only we could understand why it is that we're here and what it is that we're meant to spend our lives doing. I am uncertain when it comes to a great many things. But there is now one thing I am defiantly certain of.

Roland folds up the piece of paper, puts it back in his pocket and – from another pocket – takes out a small black box.

Marianne Roland, please.

Roland kneels and opens the small black box.

Roland, get up, come on.

Roland Marianne Aubele, will you marry me?

Beat.

Marianne Roland, we talked about this. Come on.

Roland stands and returns the small black box to his pocket.

Marianne This is a surprise.

Roland Is it?

Marianne It's the middle of the afternoon.

49

Roland There's something I'd like to say to you.

Roland reaches into a pocket, but there is nothing there.

Shit.

Marianne What is it?

Roland checks his other pockets.

Roland I've left it at home.

Marianne Left what at home? Roland.

Beat.

Roland, is everything all right?

Roland Okay I'm gonna just – I'm gonna just own up: I came down here because I wanted to – I had this whole speech written out. Took me a fucking age. And it's – It's just thrown me a bit.

Marianne Roland you're sweating.

Roland There's something I'd like to say. To you.

Roland readies himself to speak.

Um, so, as you know, well, maybe, *maybe* you know, there are, there are three different kinds of bees. There's the drones, there's the workers and there's the queen. And the, the drones are all women. Sorry, the, the workers, the *workers* are all women. The drones have sex with the queen. But then once they've, once they've ejaculated, they, er, they die. Shoulda written this down.

Marianne Roland –

Roland What I'm tryina say is that bees have a really short life. They have an incredibly short life and then that's it. Possibly the bit about the life span shoulda come at the start and then I coulda moved on to the –

Marianne Is there something –

Roland Do you remember when we first met?

Marianne Yes.

Roland You do?

Marianne Yes.

Roland At that wedding.

Marianne What?

Roland John and Ruth's wedding.

Marianne We met at a barbecue.

Roland takes a piece of A4 paper from a pocket and reads.

Roland There are three different kinds of bees. The drones, the workers and a single, solitary queen. The workers are all women. Their job is to forage for honey, pollen, etcetera. Their lifespan is potentially anywhere between five weeks and six months. And then they die. Drones exist solely to have sex with the queen. Each hive tends to have around a hundred drones. Once they've deposited their sperm, their penis gets ripped off and they die. Honeybees have an unfailing clarity of purpose. Their lives are often intensely short. But in a strange sort of way, I'm jealous of the humble honeybee and their quiet elegance. If only our existence were that simple. If only we could understand why it is that we're here and what it is that we're meant to spend our lives doing. I am uncertain when it comes to a great many things. But there is now one thing I am defiantly certain of.

Roland folds up the piece of paper, puts it back in his pocket and – from another pocket – takes out a small black box. He kneels and opens the small black box.

Roland Marianne Aubele, will you marry me?

Marianne Okay.

Roland Really?

Marianne Yeah, really.

Marianne kisses Roland. Roland slides the engagement ring on to the appropriate finger. Marianne kisses Roland.

Where was that speech from? Was it from a book? It was, wasn't it? Was it the Ted Hooper? It was, wasn't it?

Roland Bits.

Marianne laughs and then kisses Roland.

Marianne I've got to do a fucking tutorial.

Roland I'll see you at home.

Marianne Is that okay?

Roland Of course.

Marianne Thank you.

Marianne kisses Roland.

Marianne *If you're serious you write to them.*

Roland *Meaning what?*

Marianne *Outline why they ought to be taking you seriously.*

Roland *And if they do?*

Marianne *You meet someone.*

Roland *Out there or here?*

Marianne *Out there. You*

You

You have to meet them a couple of times.

Roland *Always out there?*

Marianne *I think so.*

Roland *Then what?*

Marianne *Then it's up to you.*

Roland *How do they do it, how does it work?*

Marianne *They use something called a Bar*

Abar

A

A

Roland *It's okay.*

Marianne *They mix it with water.*

Roland *I don't really know what to say.*

Marianne *You don't have to say anything.*

Roland *No I know but I want to; I want to know what to say to you.*

Marianne *A lot of people apparently never go through with it.*

Roland *How do you mean?*

Marianne *A lot of people, once they've been given the green night*

Night

Once they've   A lot of

Roland *It's okay.*

Marianne *They're, they're happy enough knowing it's there.*

Roland How bad is it? Mary –

Marianne It's pretty bad.

Roland How bad is pretty bad?

Marianne They said being under forty might help, but –

Roland Mary, how bad is pretty bad?

Marianne I'm not sure I want to talk about it right away.

Roland Mary I've been waiting around on tenterhooks.

Marianne I'm not sure I *can* talk about it right away.

Roland Do you want something to drink, do you want some water?

Marianne No thank you.

Roland Do you want some booze, I mean –

Marianne I'm just after a moment's silence and then I'll tell you anything you want.

Beat.

He said, I think, something like a third, a third of people live for a year.

Roland What about the other two?

Marianne What?

Roland What about the other two-thirds, how long do they –

Marianne I don't know, Roland, I don't know.

Roland What did they tell you, what did the –

Marianne I don't – I don't know. I can't remember. They gave me some leaflets. I mean fuck me, why does it matter what happens to the other two-thirds?

Roland Why does it matter?

Marianne Yes.

Roland It matters because presumably we don't know which third you're going to be?

Marianne Why are you being arsey with me –

Roland I'm not being –

Marianne Yes you are, you're being arsey. You're getting mad at me for not remembering this number or that number – I mean who gives a fuck –

Roland All right –

Marianne I'll go upstairs and get my fucking handbag and you can rifle through the plethora of leaflets if it bothers you that fucking –

Roland All right. All right. I'm sorry. I'm sorry. Did he talk about treatment?

Marianne He said they can operate. Try and remove it, remove as much of it as they can. Then they said radiotherapy but if I'm too weak for radiotherapy, they said chemo. Shitload of chemo. It's right at the front.

Roland The front?

Marianne It's all over the frontal lobe.

Roland I don't know what that means.

Marianne He said I might have trouble selecting words. Selecting the right words. He said I should expect seizures.

Roland Jesus Christ.

Marianne It's palliative. Whatever they do. It's not – They can't.

Roland Okay.

Marianne They said this is it.

Roland Okay.

Marianne This is it, they said.

Roland Okay. Okay.

Marianne Why don't you sit down?

Roland I need to sit down, do I?

Marianne Maybe. I mean. No, standing is fine.

Roland I would have come with you if you'd told me, you know.

Marianne I know.

Roland I would've cancelled –

Marianne I know. I wanted to go alone.

Roland I'm a bit angry actually, Mary.

Marianne Angry?

Roland I'm saying so that you know.

Marianne You're angry?

Roland I'm saying so that you know because I don't want to have an argument.

Marianne Glad to fucking hear it.

Roland All right.

Marianne I'm sorry you missed out on the sheer joy that was collecting the results of my biopsy, Roland.

Roland All right.

Marianne But, forgive me, I didn't feel like inviting along a fucking entourage of onlookers.

Roland All right! Christ. I'm telling you so I can get it off my chest because I want to be as honest with you as I possibly can. Because I don't know what you're about to say but it's clearly bad news and I want to be able to listen and not be thinking I wonder what she did with herself once she heard?

Marianne The reason –

Roland I wonder why she didn't call me straight away?

Marianne I knew that you were –

Roland Because I would have dropped absolutely anything and everything and I wonder if she knows that?

Marianne So I got my biopsy results.

Roland Today?

Marianne They called me and asked me to come in.

Roland Who did you see?

Marianne Dr Thorne.

Roland What did he say?

Marianne He said it's benign.

Roland What?

Marianne He said that it's a grade one and he said that it's benign.

Roland Wait, he said that –

Marianne He said that, ordinarily, with a grade one he would expect to see a full recovery.

Roland Did he use the phrase 'full recovery'?

Marianne Exact quote.

Roland He said –

Marianne Ordinarily we would expect to see a full recovery.

Roland Fucking hell.

Marianne Yeah.

Roland What happens now?

Marianne They need to operate.

Roland But he definitely used the phrase 'full recovery'?

Marianne He did.

   Beat.

Roland Are you all right?

Marianne Yeah.

Roland Are you sure?

Marianne Yeah.

Roland Are you hungry, do you want some bolognaise? Home-made.

Marianne Have we got any of the nice spaghetti?

Roland I love you.

Marianne It's called a glioblastoma multiforme.

Roland Right.

Marianne It's a grade four.

Roland Right.

Marianne It's at the front.

Roland Okay.

Marianne Which is why I've been having trouble –

Roland Speaking.

Marianne He said he thinks they should operate.

Roland Great.

Marianne He said he thinks that's what they should start with.

Roland Great.

Marianne And then he suggested radiotherapy.

Roland Okay.

Marianne But he said that if I'm too weak for radiotherapy –

Roland Too weak?

Marianne Yes.

Roland Okay, sorry.

Marianne He said that if I'm too weak for radiotherapy then chemo is probably better.

Roland Okay.

Marianne He . . . he said that . . .

Roland We can stop.

Marianne No, I'm okay.

Roland We could eat.

Marianne No, I'm fine.

Roland Honestly, we can stop, we can eat.

Marianne Think I'd rather. Think I'd rather just get –

Roland No, you're right –

Marianne Think I'd rather just get through it.

Roland Absolutely.

Marianne It's a year.

Roland A year?

Marianne Probably less.

Roland It's probably less than a year?

Marianne He didn't say that, but.

Roland They didn't say that?

Marianne I went online.

Roland But they didn't tell you that?

Marianne They said we should talk about all of that when we next meet, but when I got back to campus –

Roland Mary –

Marianne I know, I know. It's stupid. I shouldn't have done it. I went on a forum.

Roland A forum?

Marianne People had left all these dedications to all these people they had known that had died. There were pages and pages of them. Most of them were really wet and drippy. I got really fucking angry.

Roland Angry?

Marianne There's so much bullshit.

Roland You mean on the –

Marianne When someone dies.

Roland Right.

Marianne There's so much bullshit. 'When your time's up your time's up.'

Roland Right.

Marianne *'Time'*, I mean what on earth are they even talking about?

Roland Why don't we –

Marianne 'She was a real fighter.' Was she? Well, she obviously didn't do a very good fucking job, did she?

Roland All right.

Marianne Some of them had uploaded photos.

Roland We should eat.

Marianne There was a photograph of a woman with God knows how many tubes hanging out of her and she was surrounded by these garish fucking balloons.

Roland Some people like to give people balloons.

Marianne If you give me a balloon, I will fucking garotte you.

Roland Note to self.

Marianne And if you put a photo of me on a fucking forum, I will haunt the shit out of you.

Roland No forums.

Marianne goes to cry, but stops herself.

Okay. Let's eat. We should eat.

Marianne and Roland use sign language for the following lines.

Marianne It's a kind of cancer. A kind of tumour.

Roland Okay.

Marianne It's at the front.

Roland Okay.

Marianne It's the reason I've been having trouble typing.

Roland I understand.

Marianne The doctor thinks they should operate.

Roland Good.

Marianne Operation to start with.

Roland Great.

Marianne Then he suggested radiotherapy.

Roland Okay.

Marianne But he said that if I'm too weak for radiotherapy then chemo is probably better. It's a year.

Roland A year?

Marianne Might be less.

Roland Less than a year?

Marianne Yes.

Roland Less than one year of your life to live?

Marianne Wasn't specific.

Roland What did the doctor say?

Marianne I went online.

Roland Who said less than one year?

Marianne They said we should talk about all of that when we next meet, but when I got back to campus, I went on a forum.

Roland A forum?

Marianne Yes.

Roland Why did you go on to a forum?

Marianne People had left all these dedications to all these people they had known that had died. There were pages and pages of them. Most of them were really wet and drippy. I got really angry.

Roland Angry?

Marianne There's so much crap.

Roland What do you mean?

Marianne When someone dies.

Roland Right.

Marianne There's so much crap. 'When your time's up your time's up.'

Roland Right.

Marianne 'She was a real fighter.' Was she? Well, she obviously didn't do a very good fucking job, did she?

Roland All right.

Marianne Some of them had uploaded photos.

Roland We should have something to eat.

Marianne There was a photograph of a woman with God knows how many tubes hanging out of her and she was surrounded by these garish fucking balloons.

Roland Some people like to give people balloons.

Marianne If you give me a balloon, I will fucking garotte you.

Roland Note to self.

Marianne And if you put a photo of me on a fucking forum, I will haunt the shit out of you.

Roland No forums.

Marianne goes to cry, but stops herself.

Why don't we have something to eat?

Marianne *I think I'd like to go abroad.*

Roland *What do you mean?*

Marianne *I'm not. I'm not sure how much of a difference the chemo is really making.*

Roland *D'you mean you're not sure or they're not sure?*

Marianne *I mean me. I mean I'm not sure.*

Roland *Why? What aren't you sure about, why aren't you sure?*

Marianne *It's ganging*

It's

It's

I was coming home. I was on the train and I was c-coming home. A group of men got on. A group of thirty-year-old men. They were pissed. I was sat at a table and I had my laptop out. They sat at my table and the table opposite. They started, they started winding me up. I put my laptop in my bag and I tried to move to a different seat. But they blocked me, they wouldn't let me past. I couldn't speak. I couldn't find the right words and they started laughing. They howled with laughter. I started to cry and finally one of them said that's enough.

64

Roland *You should have said, you should have told me.*

Marianne *I went on to campus.*

Roland *What do you mean, what for?*

Marianne *To have lunch with Melisa. I had a seizure.*

Roland *What? When? Mary.*

Marianne *A couple of weeks ago.*

Roland *A couple of weeks ago?*

Marianne *Yes.*

Roland *Why didn't you tell me?*

Marianne *It's the words, Roland. It's exhibit*

It's ex

It's becoming more and more   tiring.

Roland *You mean speaking to me, the two of us, is tiring, or you mean everything?*

Marianne *I mean everything.*

Roland *I didn't realise.*

Marianne *I know.*

Roland *I'm sorry.*

Marianne *I know.*

Roland *I don't know what to do.*

Marianne *You don't have to do anything.*

Roland *I want to help.*

Marianne *You are.*

Roland *So when you say abroad, you mean abroad and not come back?*

Marianne *Potentially   yes.*

Roland *How does it work?*

Marianne *You become a member.*

Roland *A member?*

Marianne *Pay some money.*

Roland *How much?*

Marianne *I don't know what it is in pounds.*

Roland *Then what?*

Marianne *If you're serious you write to them.*

Roland *Meaning what?*

Marianne *Outline why they ought to be taking you seriously.*

Roland *And if they do?*

Marianne *You meet someone.*

Roland *Out there or here?*

Marianne *Out there. You*

You

You have to meet them a couple of times.

Roland *Always out there?*

Marianne *I think so.*

Roland *Then what?*

Marianne *Then it's up to you.*

Roland *How do they do it, how does it work?*

Marianne *They use something called a Bar*

Abar

A

A

Roland *It's okay.*

Marianne *They mix it with water.*

Roland *I don't really know what to say.*

Marianne *You don't have to say anything.*

Roland *No I know but I want to; I want to know what to say to you.*

Marianne *A lot of people apparently never go through with it.*

Roland *How do you mean?*

Marianne *A lot of people, once they've been given the green night*

Night

Once they've   A lot of

Roland *It's okay.*

Marianne *They're, they're happy enough knowing it's there.*

Roland *How do you know that?*

Marianne *It's on the website.*

Roland *When you say a lot how many are we talking?*

Marianne *I think it was something like two-thirds. Safety net. For a lot of people.*

Roland *And is that how you're feeling about it?*

Marianne *I don't know.*

Roland *Would I be able to come with you?*

Marianne *I'm going to speak to Martin. Would you want to? Come with me.*

Roland *Would you want me to come with you?*

Marianne nods. Beat.

Marianne *I keep thinking of Mum.*

Roland *In what way?*

Marianne *Before she died.*

Roland *Right.*

Marianne *When she said she didn't want any more food.*

Roland *Yeah.*

Marianne *Do you remember?*

Roland *I'm not sure we ever really talked about it?*

Marianne *I thought we did?*

Roland *Bits and pieces maybe.*

Marianne *Well she said she wanted them to stop the IV, did we talk about that?*

Roland *I think maybe we did yeah.*

Marianne *They asked me to leave. I went back the next day and she was starting to look like a ghost. It takes an enormous amount of strength. When you're like that. To keep going. I'm not sure I have it.*

Roland *You don't know. You don't know that.*

Marianne *Sinking feeling.*

Roland *Mary listen to me –*

Marianne *I'm so tired. I'm so tired, Roland. Before people had face*

Before they had   face

Face   before they

FUCK.

Roland *Okay.*

Marianne *God.*

Roland *God?*

Marianne *People's lives were their own. Before*   *it became skin*

Skin, it became

Skin

Roland *Skin?*

Marianne *Mum wasn't scared of dying, she was scared of being kept alive. You know?*

Roland *Yes.*

Marianne *That wasn't what scared her.*

Roland *I understand.*

Marianne *It's not just the speaking.*

Roland *Okay now I don't understand?*

Marianne *Reading. I'm having trouble – Numbers, words, on the page. I don't know how to explain it. Typing. Typing, as well.*

Roland *In what way?*

Marianne *I know the word. I know the word I'm trying to type. But I don't know the letters. None of the letters seem right. Rea*

Rea

Rea

Roland *You don't need to finish.*

Marianne *I want to.*

Roland *I think I know what you're trying to say.*

Marianne *How*   *How can you know what I'm trying to say?*

Mmm   Most of the time I don't even know what I'm trying to say.

Roland *You're right I was being polite because I don't want you to wear yourself out.*

Marianne *Maybe we should get me a notepad to hang around my neck?*

Roland *What?*

Marianne *Kidding.*

Roland *Mary fucking hell.*

Marianne *Roland I don't think that I can go back to work.*

Roland *Have they told you that?*

Marianne *They're great.*

Roland *You've told them then?*

Marianne *Not yet.*

Roland *But you're going to.*

Marianne *I think so.*

Roland *But you haven't said any of this to them?*

Marianne *They've said whatever I want.*

Roland *So what about part-time?*

Marianne *I don't know the point.*

Roland *You mean the point of going part-time?*

Marianne *Either I'm walking or I'm*

Either I'm   walker

I either do it or I don't. Scares me.

Roland *Work?*

Marianne *Stopping.*

Roland *Stopping work scares you?*

Marianne *What will I do?*

Roland *We'll go away. We can do whatever we want.*

Marianne *I don't –*

Roland *I'm being serious.*

Marianne *I don't –*

Roland *I mean it.*

Marianne *I   I don't*
We can't. I have to   have to   make a
I have to have a choice.
Control.

Roland Taxi's booked for nine.

Marianne I know.

Roland Gives us an extra half an hour.

Marianne It does.

Roland Are you tired?

Marianne A bit.

Roland Would you like to go to sleep?

Marianne What time is it?

Roland Are you cold?

Marianne No.

Roland I could turn the air conditioning off?

Marianne I'm fine.

Roland Taxi's booked for nine.

Marianne I know.

Roland Gives us an extra half an hour.

Marianne It does.

Roland Are you tired?

Marianne A bit.

Roland Would you like to go to sleep?

Marianne What time is it?

Roland Are you cold?

Marianne No.

Roland I could turn the air conditioning off?

Marianne I'm fine.

Roland Taxi's booked for nine.

Marianne I know.

Roland Gives us an extra half an hour.

Marianne It does.

Roland Are you tired?

Marianne A bit.

Roland Would you like to go to sleep?

Marianne What time is it?

Roland Are you cold?

Marianne No.

Roland I could turn the air conditioning off?

Marianne I'm fine.

Roland Do you want to put the telly on?

Marianne No thank you.

Roland Are you hungry?

Marianne Full.

Roland I've. I've had a really wonderful day.

Marianne Same.

Roland Really?

Marianne Yes.

Roland Can I be honest with you?

Marianne No.

She's joking. They perhaps smile a little.

Roland There are, there are times when I look at you and I absolutely understand why you're doing this. But there are times when I absolutely don't. And I'm not, I'm not saying you shouldn't be calling it a day. But I s'pose I am starting to wonder if now is the right time. Because if it were me and I were you I think that I would want as much time as possible. And if you think you've got another couple of months in you, God I would love to give that a go.

Marianne Yes.

Roland What?

Marianne (*beat*) Yes. Let's go home.

Roland Because if it were me and I were you I think that I would want as much time as possible. And if you think you've got another couple of weeks in you, God I would love to give that a go.

Marianne What   what do you mean by time?

Roland Time, I mean time, I'd want more time. With you.

Marianne I'm not   sure   that

You and I, we might, we think that

But that, that

There's an arrow   from p-past to present.

Roland Mary –

Marianne But that's really all we can say. Asymmetrical.

Roland Mary –

Marianne But nobody knows why.

Roland Okay.

Marianne L-listen to me, please.

Roland Let's not talk about this now.

Marianne Please.

Roland I shouldn't have brought it up.

Marianne L-listen to me, please. The basic laws of physics – The b-b-basic laws of physics don't have a past and a present. Time is irrelevant at the level of a-atoms and molecules. It's symmetrical.

We have all the time we've always had.

You'll still have all our time.

Once I

Once

Once

There's not going to be any more or less of it.

Once I'm gone.

Roland Hello, Marianne.

Marianne Roland. Wow, hi – Hello. How are you?

Roland Yeah, I'm fine, thanks.

Marianne Oh good. Good, that's really good.

Roland How about y'self?

Marianne I bought some of your honey.

Roland Oh really.

Marianne From the Budgens in Crouch End.

Roland Yeah, right. They're really great.

Marianne I said to the girl on the till, I said I used to know the man who made this honey.

Roland What did she say?

Marianne She just stared at me.

Roland I read one of your papers.

Marianne You did not?

Roland I did. I downloaded it.

Marianne That's really amazing, Roland.

Roland What did you think of the honey?

Marianne Delicious. It was completely delicious. Are you, are you here for the ballroom class?

Roland Yeah, no, yeah, I am, yeah.

Marianne Really.

Roland Heather's getting married in a couple of months, so.

Marianne The PE teacher?

Roland That's right, yeah. Good memory. I've been ordered to sort out my two left feet or else. How about you?

Marianne Similar, really. Wedding.

Roland Your own or –

Marianne No, God, can you imagine. I'm being a very diligent bridesmaid. We're having some kind of mass Viennese waltz. I'm not sure I fully understand it as yet.

Roland So is this your first? Lesson.

Marianne No, second. You?

Roland First, yeah.

Marianne Well done on the comfortable trouser front. I came straight from work. Last week. Crotch was like a fucking hothouse by the time I got home.

Beat.

Roland We should – Afterwards – If you – If we're not both completely exhausted. There's a nice place not that far. We could – We could try going for a drink? But if we get there, if we're there, if we're there and you, you change your mind, if you change your mind and you wanna call it a day, then we'll just call it a day. We'll just call it a day and you'll never have to see me again.